Stanley at School

Written by
Linda Bailey

Illustrated by
Bill Slavin

KIDS CAN PRESS

Stanley knew he wasn't supposed to go into the school. School was for kids. Dogs had to stay outside.

But the school was right there! On Stanley's street! Every morning, the kids walked past his yard to go in. Every afternoon, they walked past again to go home.

And every day, Stanley got more and more curious. What did the kids *do* in that school all day?

He asked his friends at the dog park.

"School?" said Alice in dog talk. "Is *that* where they go?"

"I'd like to see that school," said Nutsy.

"I'd like to *sniff* it," barked Gassy Jack.

So the very next day, they all snuck out of their yards.

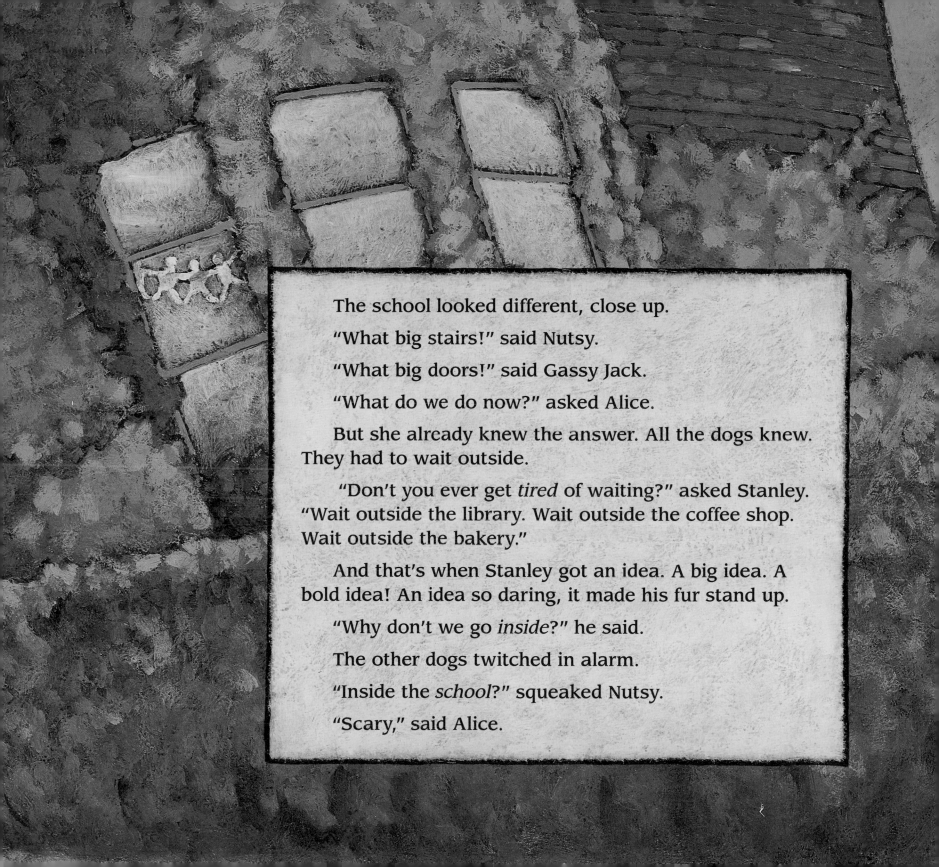

The school looked different, close up.

"What big stairs!" said Nutsy.

"What big doors!" said Gassy Jack.

"What do we do now?" asked Alice.

But she already knew the answer. All the dogs knew. They had to wait outside.

"Don't you ever get *tired* of waiting?" asked Stanley. "Wait outside the library. Wait outside the coffee shop. Wait outside the bakery."

And that's when Stanley got an idea. A big idea. A bold idea! An idea so daring, it made his fur stand up.

"Why don't we go *inside*?" he said.

The other dogs twitched in alarm.

"Inside the *school*?" squeaked Nutsy.

"Scary," said Alice.

But Stanley was already running up the stairs.

"Follow me!" he barked.

It wasn't easy to get four dogs through the big school doors. But with a bit of thinking, and a lot of pushing, they figured it out.

Alice was right. It *was* scary in there. Everywhere they looked was empty. Everywhere they listened was quiet.

"What have they done to the kids?" yipped Nutsy.

Gassy Jack sniffed the air. "They're in here somewhere. I can smell 'em."

All the dogs took deep sniffs. The air in that school was *thick* with great smells. Socks. Hamster poop. Chalk. And something else ...

... something that made the dogs drool.

"Does anyone else smell salami?" asked Stanley. He could hardly believe his nose!

They followed the trail, and what did they find? A room full of jackets and backpacks all stuffed full of ...

LUNCH!

And, oh, what a lunch it was ... cheese sticks and cherry pies, chow mein and chicken. The food in that school was divine. And the dogs ate it up, every bit.

Even the pickles!

And just when things couldn't get better ...

... they did.

Because that's when the kids showed up!

Those dogs were so happy, their whole bodies wagged.
They *loved* kids. Kids chased balls, they dug holes, they
rolled in the grass. Kids were almost as good as dogs.

So the dogs barked, and the kids laughed, and there
was more fun than a box full of puppies.

Right up till they noticed ...

... the man with the broom.

Stanley didn't understand people talk. But he could tell what the man was saying.

"Bad dogs!"

There was only one thing to do.

"RUN!" barked Stanley.

He tore off down the hall. Behind him came his friends. And behind *them* came the kids!

They ran through a room full of bouncy balls.

They ran through a room full of noisy things.

They ran through a room
full of wet stuff ...

... and into a room that had

NO WAY OUT!

That's when a hand clamped down on Stanley's collar. Other hands grabbed his friends. Quick as a lick, they were sitting on cold, hard chairs.

The only thing those dogs smelled now was trouble.

"Uh-oh," whimpered Nutsy. "Who's that?"

Stanley thought he knew. "The top dog," he said.

"She's not a dog," said Alice.

"Maybe not," said Stanley, "but she's the top dog *here*."

They waited … and waited … and waited some more. The waiting was terrible!

"I say we make a run for it," said Gassy Jack.

"Too late," said Stanley. "Here she comes."

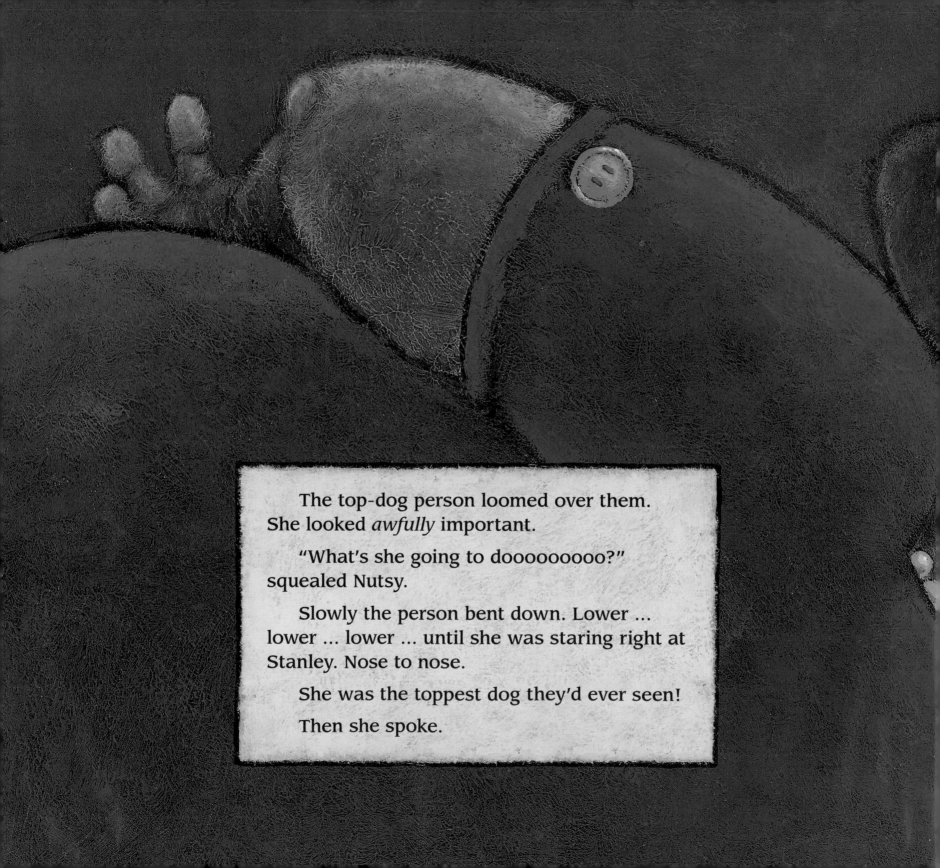

The top-dog person loomed over them. She looked *awfully* important.

"What's she going to dooooooooo?" squealed Nutsy.

Slowly the person bent down. Lower ... lower ... lower ... until she was staring right at Stanley. Nose to nose.

She was the toppest dog they'd ever seen!

Then she spoke.

"There now, my sweeties," she crooned in a soft, gentle voice. "There, there, there." And she patted Nutsy's head.

She patted the other dogs, too.

For a long time, the dogs just sat there, making happy, grunty sounds as their heads got plenty of pats.

Finally the top-dog person stood up.

"Off!" she said.

The dogs hopped off the chairs.

"Come!" she said.

The dogs came. They followed her in a tidy dog line.

"Go!" she said and opened the big door as if it were nothing.

The dogs went.

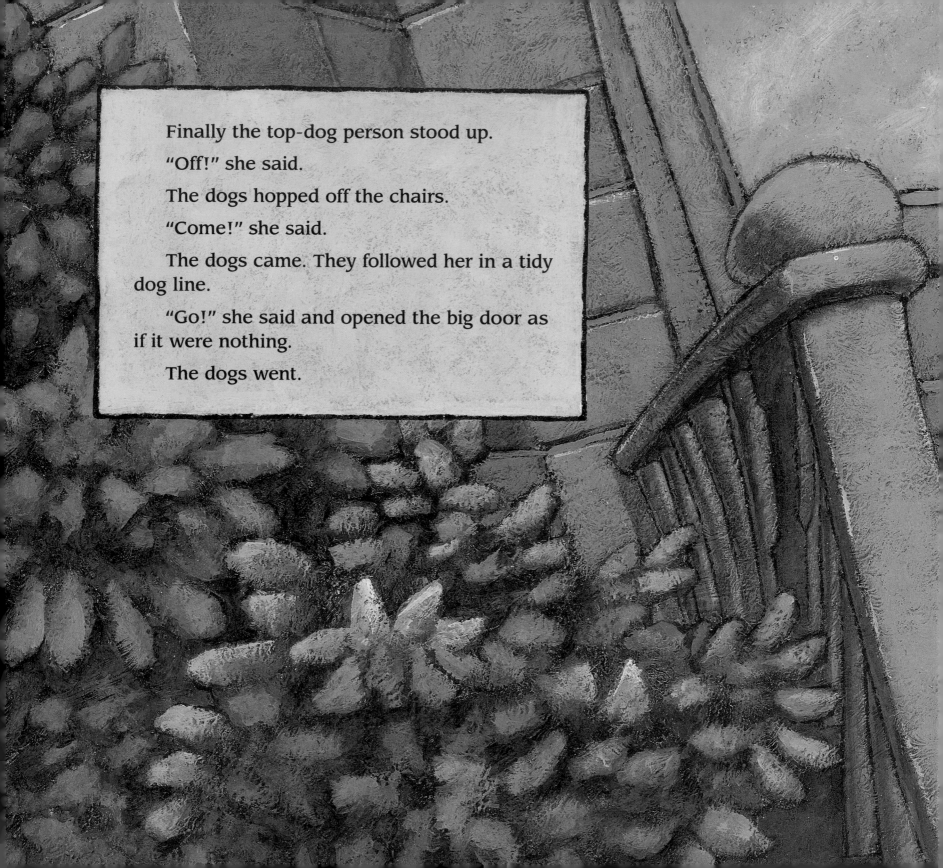

They stayed in their dog line for two whole blocks.

"Wrow!" said Nutsy when they stopped. "That school was amazing."

"What an exciting place!" said Alice. "And just think. The kids go there every day."

"And now we know why," said Gassy Jack.

"Yup," said Stanley. "They go there to eat and to run."

"Yup," agreed the others. "Eat and run. *That's* what the kids do in school."

Now that they'd figured it out, the dogs felt extremely clever.

And later when they went to the dog park, they were still talking about that school. And maybe they told a few friends about the eating and the running. And maybe there were other dogs who'd been wondering what kids do all day.

All I know is, when the school doors opened the next morning ...

... the dogs were waiting!

For Sasha, Miles and Esmé,
who know how to have fun! — L.B.

For Bridget and all of her kids at Dundurn — B.S.

Text © 2015 Linda Bailey
Illustrations © 2015 Bill Slavin

Kids Can Press acknowledges the financial support of the Government
of Ontario, through the Ontario Media Development Corporation's Ontario Book Initiative;
the Ontario Arts Council; the Canada Council for the Arts; and the Government of Canada,
through the CBF, for our publishing activity.

Published in Canada by
Kids Can Press Ltd.
25 Dockside Drive
Toronto, ON M5A 0B5

Published in the U.S. by
Kids Can Press Ltd.
2250 Military Road
Tonawanda, NY 14150

www.kidscanpress.com

The artwork in this book was rendered in acrylics, on gessoed paper.
The text is set in Leawood Medium.

Edited by Debbie Rogosin
Designed by Julia Naimska

This book is smyth sewn casebound.
Manufactured in Tseung Kwan O, NT Hong Kong, China,
in 3/2015 by Paramount Printing Co. Ltd.

CM 15 0 9 8 7 6 5 4 3 2 1

Library and Archives Canada Cataloguing in Publication

Bailey, Linda, 1948–, author
Stanley at school / written by Linda Bailey ; illustrated
by Bill Slavin.

ISBN 978-1-77138-096-6 (bound)

I. Slavin, Bill, illustrator II. Title.

PS8553.A3644S715 2015   jC813'.54   C2014-906930-8

Kids Can Press is a *corus*™ Entertainment company